THE SEISMOGRAPH
ADVENTURE

BY

ARTHUR B. REEVE

British Library Cataloguing-in-Publication Data
A catalogue record for this book is available from the
British Library

Arthur Benjamin Reeve

Arthur Benjamin Reeve was born on 15th October 1880 in New York, USA.

Reeve received his University education at Princeton and upon graduating enrolled at the New York Law School. However, his career was not destined to be in the field of Law. Between 1910 and 1918 he produced 82 short stories for Cosmopolitan magazine featuring his super-sleuth Professor Craig Kennedy. Kennedy is sometimes referred to as "The American Sherlock Holmes" due to his astounding ability at crime solving and his Watson-like sidekick Walter Jameson, a newspaper reporter. These characters featured in 18 novels, some of which were pseudo-novels stitched together from various short stories.

During this period he also began authoring screenplays, beginning with *The Exploits of Elaine* (1914). By the end of this decade his film career was at its peak with his name appearing on seven films, most of them serials and three of them starring Harry Houdini. Due to the film industry's migration to the west coast of America and Reeve's desire to remain in the east he produced less and less work for film. However, in 1927 he entered into a contract to write film scenarios for notorious millionaire-murderer, Harry K. Thaw, on the subject of fake spiritualists. The deal resulted in a lawsuit when Thaw refused to pay. In late 1928, Reeve declared bankruptcy.

Reeve continued to write detective stories for pulp magazines, but also covered many celebrated crime cases for various newspapers, including the murder of William Desmond Taylor, and the trial of Lindbergh baby kidnapper, Bruno Hauptmann. During the 1930s he became an anti-rackets crusader and produced a work of history on the subject titled *The Golden Age of Crime* (1931).

In 1932 he moved to Trenton to be near his alma mater. He died on 9th August 1936.

THE SEISMOGRAPH ADVENTURE

"Dr. James Hanson, Coroner's Physician, Criminal Courts Building," read Craig Kennedy, as he held a visitor's card in his hand. Then to the visitor he added, "Take a chair, Doctor."

The physician thanked him and sat down. "Professor Kennedy," he began, "I have been referred to you by Inspector O'Connor of the Detective Bureau. It may seem an impertinence for a city official to call on you for assistance, but—well, you see, I'm completely floored. I think, too, that the case will interest you. It's the Vandam case."

If Dr. Hanson had suddenly turned on the current of an induction coil and I had been holding the handles I don't think the thrill I received could have been any more sudden. The Vandam case was the sensation of the moment, a triple puzzle, as both Kennedy and myself had agreed. Was it suicide, murder, or sudden death? Every theory, so far, had proved unsatisfactory.

"I have read only what the newspapers have published," replied Craig to the doctor's look of inquiry. "You see, my friend Jameson here is on the staff of the Star, and we are in the habit of discussing these cases."

"Very glad to meet you, Mr. Jameson," exclaimed Dr. Hanson at the implied introduction. "The relations between my office and your paper have always been very satisfactory, I can assure you."

"Thank you, Doctor. Depend on me to keep them so," I replied, shaking his proffered hand.

"Now, as to the case," continued the doctor slowly. "Here is a beautiful woman in the prime of life, the wife of a very wealthy retired banker considerably older than herself— perhaps nearly seventy—of very fine family. Of course you have read it all, but let me sketch it so you will look at it from my point of view. This woman, apparently in good health, with every luxury money can buy, is certain within a very few years, from her dower rights, to be numbered among the richest women in America. Yet she is discovered in the middle of the night by her maid, seated at the table in the library of her home, unconscious. She never regains consciousness, but dies the following morning.

"The coroner is called in, and, as his physician, I must advise him. The family physician has pronounced it due to natural causes, the uremic coma of latent kidney trouble. Some of the newspapers, I think the Star among them, have hinted at suicide. And then there are others, who have flatly asserted it was murder."

The coroner's physician paused to see if we were following him. Needless to say Kennedy was ahead of him.

"Have you any facts in your possession which have not been given to the public yet?" asked Craig.

"I'm coming to that in a moment," replied Dr. Hanson. "Let me sketch the case first. Henry Vandam had become— well, very eccentric in his old age, we will say. Among his eccentricities none seems to have impressed the newspapers more than his devotion to a medium and her manager, Mrs. May Popper and Mr. Howard Farrington. Now, of course, the case does not go into the truth or falsity of spiritualism, you understand. You have your opinion, and I have mine. What this aspect of the case involves is merely the character of the medium and her manager. You know, of course, that Henry Vandam is completely under their control."

He paused again, to emphasise the point.

"You asked me if I was in possession of any facts which have not been given to the press. Yes, I am. And just there lies the trouble. They are so very conflicting as to be almost worse than useless, as far as I can see. We found near the unfortunate woman a small pill-box with three capsules still in it. It was labelled 'One before retiring' and bore the name of a certain druggist and the initials 'Dr. C. W. H.' Now, I am convinced that the initials are merely a blind and do not give any clue. The druggist says that a maid from the Vandam house brought in the prescription, which of course he filled. It is a harmless enough prescription—contains, among other things, four and a half grains of quinine and one-sixth of a grain of morphine. Six capsules were prepared altogether.

5

"Now, of course my first thought was that she might have taken several capsules at once and that it was a case of accidental morphine poisoning, or it might even be suicide. But it cannot be either, to my mind, for only three of the six capsules are gone. No doubt, also, you are acquainted with the fact that the one invariable symptom of morphine poisoning is the contraction of the pupils of the eyes to a pin-point—often so that they are unrecognisable. Moreover, the pupils are symmetrically contracted, and this symptom is the one invariably present in coma from morphine poisoning and distinguishes it from all other forms of death.

"On the other hand, in the coma of kidney disease one pupil is dilated and the other contracted—they are unsymmetrical. But in this case both the pupils are normal, or only a very little dilated, and they are symmetrical. So far we have been able to find no other poison than the slight traces of morphine remaining in the stomach after so many hours. I think you are enough of a chemist to know that no doctor would dare go on the stand and swear to death from morphine poisoning in the face of such evidence against him. The veriest tyro of an expert toxicologist could too easily confute him."

Kennedy nodded. "Have you the pill-box and the prescription?"

"I have," replied Dr. Hanson, placing them on the table.

Kennedy scrutinised them sharply. "I shall need these," he said. "Of course you understand I will take very good care of them. Is there anything else of importance?"

"Really, I don't know," said the physician dubiously. "It's rather out of my province, but perhaps you would think it important. It's mighty uncanny anyhow. Henry Vandam, as you doubtless know, was much more deeply interested in the work of this medium than was his wife. Perhaps Mrs. Vandam was a bit jealous—I don't know. But she, too, had an interest in spiritualism, though he was much more deeply influenced by Mrs. Popper than she.

"Here's the strange part of it. The old man believes so thoroughly in rappings and materialisations that he constantly keeps a notebook in his pocket in which he records all the materialisations he thinks he sees and the rappings he hears, along with the time and place. Now it so happened that on the night Mrs. Vandam was taken ill, he had retired—I believe in another part of the house, where he has a regular seance-room. According to his story, he was awakened from a profound sleep by a series of rappings. As was his custom, he noted the time at which they occurred. Something made him uneasy, and he said to his 'control'—at least this is his story:

"'John, is it about Mary?'

"Three raps answered 'yes,' the usual code.

"'What is the matter? Is she ill?'

7

"The three answering raps were so vigorous that he sprang out of bed and called for his wife's maid. The maid replied that Mrs. Vandam had not gone to bed yet, but that there was a light in the library and she would go to her mistress immediately. The next moment the house was awakened by the screams of the maid calling for help, that Mrs. Vandam was dying.

"That was three nights ago. On each of the two succeeding nights Henry Vandam says he has been awakened at precisely the same hour by a rapping, and on each night his 'control' has given him a message from his dead wife. As a man of science, I attribute the whole thing to an overwrought imagination. The original rappings may have been a mere coincidence with the fact of the condition of Mrs. Vandam. However, I give this to you for what it is worth."

Craig said nothing, but, as was his habit, shaded his eyes with the tips of his fingers, resting his elbows on the arms of his chair: "I suppose," he said, "you can give me the necessary authority to enter the Vandam house and look at the scene of these happenings?"

"Certainly," assented the physician, "but you will find it a queer place. There are spirit paintings and spirit photographs in every room, and Vandam's own part of the house—well, it's creepy, that's all I can say."

"And also I suppose you have performed an autopsy on the body and will allow me to drop into your laboratory to-morrow morning and satisfy myself on this morphine point?"

"Certainly," replied the coroner's physician, "at any time you say."

"At ten sharp, then, to-morrow I shall be there," said Craig. "It is now eight-thirty. Do you think I can see Vandam to-night? What time do these rappings occur?"

"Why, yes, you surely will be able to see him to-night. He hasn't stirred from the house since his wife died. He told me he momentarily expected messages from her direct when she had got strong enough in her new world. I believe they had some kind of a compact to that effect. The rappings come at twelve-thirty."

"Ah, then I shall have plenty of time to run over to my laboratory before seeing Mr. Vandam and get some apparatus I have in mind. No, Doctor, you needn't bother to go with me. Just give me a card of introduction. I'll see you to-morrow at ten. Good-night—oh, by the way, don't give out any of the facts you have told me."

"Jameson," said Craig, when we were walking rapidly over toward the university, "this promises to be an uncommonly difficult case."

"As I view it now," I said, "I have suspicions of everybody concerned in it. Even the view of the Star, that it is a case of suicide due to overwrought nerves, may explain it."

"It might even be a natural death," Craig added. "And that would make it a greater mystery than ever—a case for psychical research. One thing that I am going to do to-night will tell me much, however."

At the laboratory he unlocked a glass case and took out a little instrument which looked like two horizontal pendulums suspended by fine wires. There was a large magnet near each pendulum, and the end of each pendulum bore a needle which touched a circular drum driven by clock-work. Craig fussed with and adjusted the apparatus, while I said nothing, for I had long ago learned that in applying a new apparatus to doing old things Craig was as dumb as an oyster, until his work was crowned with success.

We had no trouble in getting in to see Mr. Vandam in his seance-room. His face was familiar to me, for I had seen him in public a number of times, but it looked strangely altered. He was nervous, and showed his age very perceptibly.

It was as the coroner's physician had said. The house was littered with reminders of the cult, books, papers, curious daubs of paintings handsomely framed, and photographs; hazy overexposures, I should have called them, but Mr. Vandam took great pride in them, and Kennedy quite won him over by his admiration for them.

They talked about the rappings, and the old man explained where and when they occurred. They proceeded from a little cabinet or closet at one end of the room. It was evident that he was a thorough believer in them and in the messages they conveyed.

Craig carefully noted everything about the room and then fell to admiring the spirit photographs, if such they might be called.

"The best of all I do not display, they are too precious," said the old man. "Would you like to see them?"

Craig assented eagerly, and Vandam left us for a moment to get them. In an instant Craig had entered the cabinet, and in a dark corner on the floor he deposited the mechanism he had brought from the laboratory. Then he resumed his seat, shutting the box in which he had brought the mechanism, so that it would not appear that he had left anything about the room.

Artfully he led the conversation along lines that interested the old man until he seemed to forget the hour. Not so, Craig. He knew it was nearing half-past twelve. The more they talked the more uncanny did this house and room of spirits seem to me. In fact, I was rapidly reaching the point where I could have sworn that once or twice something incorporeal brushed by me. I know now that it was purely imagination, but it shows what tricks the imagination can play on us.

Rap! rap! rap! rap! rap!

Five times came a curiously hollow noise from the cabinet. If it had been possible I should certainly have fled, it was so sudden and unexpected. The hall clock downstairs struck the half-hour in those chimes written by Handel for St. Paul's.

Craig leaned over to me and whispered hoarsely, "Keep perfectly still—don't move a hand or foot."

The old man seemed utterly to have forgotten us. "Is that you, John?" he asked expectantly.

Rap! rap! rap! came the reply.

"Is Mary strong enough to speak to me to-night?"

Rap! rap!

"Is she happy?"

Rap! rap!

"What makes her unhappy? What does she want? Will you spell it out?"

Rap! rap! rap!

Then, after a pause, the rapping started slowly, and distinctly to spell out words. It was so weird and uncanny that I scarcely breathed. Letter after letter the message came, nineteen raps for "s," eight for "h," five for "e," according to the place in the alphabet, numerically, of the required letter. At last it was complete.

"She thinks you are not well. She asks you to have that prescription filled again."

"Tell her I will do it to-morrow morning. Is there anything else?"

Rap! rap! came back faintly:

"John, John, don't go yet," pleaded the old man earnestly. It was easy to see how thoroughly he believed in "John," as perhaps well he might after the warning of his wife's death three nights before. "Won't you answer one other question?"

Fainter, almost imperceptibly, came a rap! rap!

For several minutes the old man sat absorbed in thought, trance-like. Then, gradually, he seemed to realise that we were in the room with him. With difficulty he took up the thread of the conversation where the rappings had broken it.

"We were talking about the photographs," he said slowly. "I hope soon to get one of my wife as she is now that she is transfigured. John has promised me one soon."

He was gathering up his treasures preparatory to putting them back in their places of safekeeping. The moment he was out of the room Craig darted into the cabinet and replaced his mechanism in the box. Then he began softly to tap the walls. At last he found the side that gave a noise similar to that which we had heard, and he seemed pleased to have found it, for he hastily sketched on an old envelope a plan of that part of the house, noting on it the location of the side of the cabinet.

Kennedy almost dragged me back to our apartment, he was in such a hurry to examine the apparatus at his leisure. He turned on all the lights, took the thing out of its case, and stripped off the two sheets of ruled paper wound around the two revolving drums. He laid them flat on the table and studied them for some minutes with evidently growing satisfaction.

At last he turned to me and said, "Walter, here is a ghost caught in the act."

I looked dubiously at the irregular up-and-down scrawl on the paper, while he rang up the Homicide Bureau of the Central Office and left word for O'Connor to call him up the first thing in the morning.

Still eyeing with satisfaction the record traced on the sheets of paper, he lighted a cigarette in a matter-of-fact way and added: "It proves to be a very much flesh-and-blood ghost, this 'John.' It walked up to the wall back of that cabinet, rapped, listened to old Vandam, rapped some more, got the answer it wanted, and walked deliberately away. The cabinet, as you may have noticed, is in a corner of the room with one side along the hallway. The ghost must have been in the hall."

"But who was it?"

"Not so fast, Walter," laughed Craig. "Isn't it enough for one night that we have found out that much?"

Fortunately I was tired, or I certainly should have dreamed of rappings and of "John" that night. I was awakened early by Kennedy talking with someone over the telephone. It was Inspector O'Connor.

Of course I heard only one side of the conversation, but as near as I could gather Kennedy was asking the inspector to obtain several samples of ink for him. I had not heard the first part of the conversation, and was considerably surprised when Kennedy hung up the receiver and said:

"Vandam had the prescription filled again early this morning, and it will soon be in the hands of O'Connor. I hope I haven't spoiled things by acting too soon, but I don't want to run the risk of a double tragedy."

"Well," I said, "it is incomprehensible to me. First I suspected suicide. Then I suspected murder. Now I almost suspect a murder and a suicide. The fact is, I don't know just what I suspect. I'm like Dr. Hanson—floored. I wonder if Vandam would voluntarily take all the capsules at once in order to be with his wife?"

"One of them alone would be quite sufficient if the 'ghost' should take a notion, as I think it will, to walk in the daytime," replied Craig enigmatically. "I don't want to run any chances, as I have said. I may be wrong in my theory of the case, Walter, so let us not discuss this phase of it until I have gone a step farther and am sure of my ground. O'Connor's man will get the capsules before Vandam has a chance to take the first one, anyhow. The 'ghost' had a purpose in that message, for O'Connor tells me that Vandam's lawyer visited him yesterday and in all probability a new will is being made, perhaps has already been made."

We breakfasted in silence and later rode down to the office of Dr. Hanson, who greeted us enthusiastically.

"I've solved it at last," he cried, "and it's easy."

Kennedy looked gravely over the analysis which Dr. Hanson shoved into his hand, and seemed very much interested in the probable quantity of morphine that must have been taken to yield such an analysis. The physician had a text-book open on his desk.

"Our old ideas of the infallible test of morphine poisoning are all exploded," he said, excitedly beginning to read a passage he had marked in the book.

"'I have thought that inequality of the pupils, that is to say, where they are not symmetrically contracted, is proof that a case is not one of narcotism, or morphine poisoning. But Professor Taylor has recorded a case of morphine poisoning in which the unsymmetrical contraction occurred.'

"There, now, until I happened to run across that in one of the authorities I had supposed the symmetrical contraction of the pupils of the eyes to be the distinguishing symptom of morphine poisoning Professor Kennedy, in my opinion we can, after all, make out our case as one of morphine poisoning."

"Is that case in the book all you base your opinion on?" asked Craig with excessive politeness.

"Yes, sir," replied the doctor reluctantly.

"Well," said Kennedy quietly, "if you will investigate that case quoted from Professor Taylor, you will find that it has been proved that the patient had one glass eye."

"Then my contention collapses and she was not poisoned?"

"No, I do not say that. All I say is that expert testimony would refute us as far as we have gone. But if you will let me make a few tests of my own I can readily clear up that end of the case, I now feel sure. Let me take these samples to my laboratory."

I was surprised when we ran into Inspector O'Connor waiting for us in the corridor of the Criminal Courts Building as we left the office of the coroner's physician. He rushed up to Kennedy and shoved into his hand a pill-box in which six capsules rattled. Kennedy narrowly inspected the box, opened it, and looked thoughtfully at the six white capsules lying so innocently within.

"One of these capsules would have been worth hundreds of thousands of dollars to 'John,'" said Craig contemplatively, as he shut the box and deposited it carefully in his inside vest pocket. "I don't believe I even said good morning to you, O'Connor," he continued. "I hope I haven't kept you waiting here long. Have you obtained the samples of ink?"

"Yes, Professor. Here they are. As soon as you telephoned this morning I sent my men out separately to get them. There's the ink from the druggist, this is from the Vandam library, this is from Farrington's room, and this is from Mrs. Popper's apartment."

"Thank you, Inspector. I don't know what I'd do without your help," said Kennedy, eagerly taking four small vials from him. "Science is all right, but organisation enables science to work quickly. And quickness is the essence of this case."

During the afternoon Kennedy was very busy in his laboratory, where I found him that night after my hurried dinner, from which he was absent.

"What, is it after dinner-time?" he exclaimed, holding up a glass beaker and watching the reaction of something he poured into it from a test-tube.

"Craig, I believe that when you are absorbed in a case, you would rather work than eat. Did you have any lunch after I left you?"

"I don't think so," he replied, regarding the beaker and not his answer. "Now, Walter, old fellow, I don't want you to be offended with me, but really I can work better if you don't constantly remind me of such things as eating and sleeping. Say, do you want to help me—really?"

"Certainly. I am as interested in the case as you are, but I can't make heads or tails of it," I replied.

"Then, I wish you would look up Mrs. Popper to-night and have a private seance with her. What I want you to do particularly is to get a good idea of the looks of the room in which she is accustomed to work. I'm going to duplicate it here in my laboratory as nearly as possible. Then I want you to arrange with her for a private 'circle' here to-morrow night. Tell her it is with a few professors at the university who are interested in psychical research and that Mr. Vandam will be present. I'd rather have her come willingly than to force her to come. Incidentally watch that manager of hers, Farrington. By all means he must accompany her."

That evening I dropped casually in on Mrs. Popper. She was a woman of great brilliance and delicacy, both in her physical and mental perceptions, of exceptional vivacity and cleverness. She must have studied me more closely than I was aware of, for I believe she relied on diverting my attention whenever she desired to produce one of her really wonderful results. Needless to say, I was completely mystified by her performance. She did spirit writing that would have done credit to the immortal Slade, told me a lot of things that were true, and many more that were unverifiable or hopelessly vague. It was really worth much more than the price, and I did not need to feign the interest necessary to get her terms for a circle in the laboratory.

Of course I had to make the terms with Farrington. The first glance aroused my suspicions of him. He was shifty-eyed, and his face had a hard and mercenary look. In spite of, perhaps rather because of, my repugnance we quickly came to an agreement, and as I left the apartment I mentally resolved to keep my eye on him.

Craig came in late, having been engaged in his chemical analyses all the evening. From his manner I inferred that they had been satisfactory, and he seemed much gratified when I told him that I had arranged successfully for the seance and that Farrington would accompany the medium.

As we were talking over the case a messenger arrived with a note from O'Connor. It was written with his usual brevity: "Have just found from servants that Farrington and Mrs. P. have key to Vandam house. Wish I had known it before. House shadowed. No one has entered or left it to-night."

Craig looked at his watch. It was a quarter after one. "The ghost won't walk to-night, Walter," he said as he entered his bedroom for a much-needed rest. "I guess I was right after all in getting the capsules as soon as possible. The ghost must have flitted unobserved in there this morning directly after the maid brought them back from the druggist."

Again, the next morning, he had me out of bed bright and early. As we descended from the Sixth Avenue "L," he led me into a peculiar little shop in the shadow of the "L" structure. He entered as though he knew the place well; but, then, that air of assurance was Kennedy's stock in trade and sat very well on him.

Few people, I suppose, have ever had a glimpse of this workshop of magic and deception. This little shop of Marina's was the headquarters of the magicians of the country. Levitation and ghostly disappearing hands were on every side. The shelves in the back of the shop were full of nickel, brass, wire, wood, and papier-mache contrivances, new and strange to the eye of the uninitiated. Yet it was all as systematic as a hardware shop.

"Is Signor Marina in?" asked Craig of a girl in the first room, given up to picture post-cards. The room was as deceptive as the trade, for it was only an anteroom to the storeroom I have described above. This storeroom was also a factory, and half a dozen artisans were hard at work in it.

Yes, the signor was in, the girl replied, leading us back into the workshop. He proved to be a short man with a bland, open face and frank eyes, the very antithesis of his trade.

"I have arranged for a circle with Mrs. May Popper," began Kennedy, handing the man his card. "I suppose you know her?"

"Indeed yes," he answered. "I furnished her seance room."

"Well, I want to hire for to-night just the same sort of tables, cabinets, carpets, everything that she has—only hire, you understand, but I am willing to pay you well for them.

It is the best way to get a good sitting, I believe. Can you do it?"

The little man thought a moment, then replied: "Si, signor yes—very nearly, near enough. I would do anything for Mrs. Popper. She is a good customer. But her manager—"

"My friend here, Mr. Jameson, has had seances with her in her own apartment," interposed Craig. "Perhaps he can help you to recollect just what is necessary."

"I know very well, signor. I have the duplicate bill, the bill which was paid by that Farrington with a check from the banker Vandam. Leave it to me."

"Then you will get the stuff together this morning and have it up to my place this afternoon."

"Yes, Professor, yes. It is a bargain. I would do anything for Mrs. Popper—she is a fine woman."

Late that afternoon I rejoined Craig at his laboratory. Signor Marina had already arrived with a truck and was disposing the paraphernalia about the laboratory. He had first laid a thick black rug. Mrs. Popper very much affected black carpets, and I had noticed that Vandam's room was carpeted in black, too. I suppose black conceals everything that one oughtn't to see at a seance.

A cabinet with a black curtain, several chairs, a light deal table, several banjos, horns, and other instruments were disposed about the room. With a few suggestions from me we made a fair duplication of the hangings on the walls.

Kennedy was manifestly anxious to finish, and at last it was done.

After Marina had gone, Kennedy stretched a curtain over the end of the room farthest from the cabinet. Behind it he placed on a shelf the apparatus composed of the pendulums and magnets. The beakers and test-tubes were also on this shelf.

He had also arranged that the cabinet should be so situated that it was next a hallway that ran past his laboratory.

"To-night, Jameson," he said, indicating a spot on the hall wall just back of the cabinet, "I shall want you to bring my guests out here and do a little spirit rapping—I'll tell you just what to do when the time comes."

That night, when we gathered in the transformed laboratory, there were Henry Vandam, Dr. Hanson, Inspector O'Connor, Kennedy, and myself. At last the sound of wheels was heard, and Mrs. Popper drove up in a hansom, accompanied by Farrington. They both inspected the room narrowly and seemed satisfied. I had, as I have said, taken a serious dislike to the man, and watched him closely. I did not like his air of calm assurance.

The lights were switched off, all except one sixteen-candle-power lamp in the farthest corner, shaded by a deep-red globe. It was just light enough to see to read very, large print with difficulty.

Mrs. Popper began immediately with the table. Kennedy and I sat on her right and left respectively, in the circle, and held her hands and feet. I confess to a real thrill when I felt the light table rise first on two legs, then on one, and finally remain suspended in the air, whence it dropped with a thud, as if someone had suddenly withdrawn his support.

The medium sat with her back to the curtain of the cabinet, and several times I could have sworn that a hand reached out and passed close to my head. At least it seemed so. The curtain bulged at times, and a breeze seemed to sweep out from the cabinet.

After some time of this sort of work Craig led gradually up to a request for a materialisation of the control of Vandam, but Mrs. Popper refused. She said she did not feel strong enough, and Farrington put in a hasty word that he, too, could feel that "there was something working against them." But Kennedy was importunate and at last she consented to see if "John" would do some rapping, even if he could not materialise.

Kennedy asked to be permitted to put the questions.

"Are you the 'John' who appears to Mr. Vandam every night at twelve-thirty?"

Rap! rap! rap! came the faint reply from the cabinet. Or rather it seemed to me to come from the floor near the cabinet, and perhaps to be a trifle muffled by the black carpet.

24

"Are you in communication with Mrs. Vandam?"

Rap! rap! rap!

"Can she be made to rap for us?"

Rap! rap!

"Will you ask her a question and spell out her answer?"

Rap! rap! rap!

Craig paused a moment to frame the question, then shot it out point-blank: "Does Mrs. Vandam know now in the other world whether anyone in this room substituted a morphine capsule for one of those ordered by her three days before she died? Does she know whether the same person has done the same thing with those later ordered by Mr. Vandam?"

"John" seemed considerably perturbed at the mention of capsules. It was a long time before any answer was forthcoming. Kennedy was about to repeat the question when a faint sound was heard.

Rap!——

Suddenly came a wild scream. It was such a scream as I had never heard before in my life. It came as though a dagger had been thrust into the heart of Mrs. Popper. The lights flashed up as Kennedy turned the switch.

A man was lying flat on the floor—it was Inspector O'Connor. He had succeeded in slipping noiselessly, like a snake, below the curtain into the cabinet. Craig had told him to look out for wires or threads stretched from Mrs. Popper's clothing to the bulging curtain of the cabinet. Imagine his surprise when he saw that she had simply freed her foot from the shoe, which I was carefully holding down, and with a backward movement of the leg was reaching out into the cabinet behind her chair and was doing the rapping with her toes.

Lying on the floor he had grasped her foot and caught her heel with a firm hand. She had responded with a wild yell that showed she knew she was trapped. Her secret was out.

Hysterically Mrs. Popper began to upbraid the inspector as he rose to his feet, but Farrington quickly interposed.

"Something was working against us to-night, gentlemen. Yet you demanded results. And when the spirits will not come, what is she to do? She forgets herself in her trance; she produces, herself, the things that you all could see supernaturally if you were in sympathy."

The mere sound of Farrington's voice seemed to rouse in me all the animosity of my nature. I felt that a man who could trump up an excuse like that when a person was caught with the goods was capable of almost anything.

"Enough of this fake seance," exclaimed Craig. "I have let it go on merely for the purpose of opening the eyes of a certain deluded gentleman in this room. Now, if you will all be seated I shall have something to say that will finally establish whether Mary Vandam was the victim of accident, suicide, or murder."

With hearts beating rapidly we sat in silence.

Craig took the beakers and test-tubes from the shelf behind the curtain and placed them on the little deal table that had been so merrily dancing about the room.

"The increasing frequency with which tales of murder by poison appear in the newspapers," he began formally, "is proof of how rapidly this new civilisation of ours is taking on the aspects of the older civilisations across the seas. Human life is cheap in this country; but the ways in which human life has been taken among us have usually been direct, simple, aboveboard, in keeping with our democratic and pioneer traditions. The pistol and the bowie-knife for the individual, the rope and the torch for the mob, have been the usual instruments of sudden death. But when we begin to use poisons most artfully compounded in order to hasten an expected bequest and remove obstacles in its way—well, we are practising an art that calls up all the memories of sixteenth century Italy.

"In this beaker," he continued, "I have some of the contents of the stomach of the unfortunate woman. The coroner's physician has found that they show traces of morphine. Was the morphine in such quantities as to be fatal? Without doubt. But equally without doubt analysis could not discover and prove it in the face of one inconsistency.

The usual test which shows morphine poisoning failed in this case. The pupils of her eyes were not symmetrically contracted. In fact they were normal.

"Now, the murderer must have known of this test. This clever criminal also knew that to be successful in the use of this drug where others had failed, the drug must be skilfully mixed with something else. In that first box of capsules there were six. The druggist compounded them correctly according to the prescription. But between the time when they came into the house from the druggist's and the time when she took the first capsule, that night, someone who had access to the house emptied one capsule of its harmless contents and refilled it with a deadly dose of morphine—a white powder which looks just like the powder already in the capsules.

"Why, then, the normal pupils of the eyes? Simply because the criminal put a little atropine, or belladonna, with the morphine. My tests show absolutely the presence of atropine, Dr. Hanson," said Craig, bowing to the physician.

"The best evidence, however, is yet to come. A second box of six capsules, all intact, was discovered yesterday in the possession of Henry Vandam. I have analysed the capsules. One contains no quinine at all—it is all morphine and atropine. It is, without doubt, precisely similar to the capsule which killed Mrs. Vandam. Another night or so, and Henry Vandam would have died the same death."

The old man groaned. Two such exposures had shaken him. He looked from one of us to another as if not knowing in whom he could trust. But Kennedy hurried on to his next point.

"Who was it that gave the prescription to Mrs. Vandam originally? She is dead and cannot tell. The others won't tell, for the person who gave her that prescription was the person who later substituted the fatal capsule in place of the harmless. The original prescription is here. I have been able to discover from it nothing at all by examining the handwriting. Nor does the texture of the paper indicate anything to me. But the ink—ah, the ink.

"Most inks seem very similar, I suppose, but to a person who has made a study of the chemical composition of ink they are very different. Ink is composed of iron tannate, which on exposure to air gives the black of writing. The original pigment—say blue or blue-black ink—is placed in the ink, to make the writing visible at first, and gradually fades, giving place to the black of the tannate which is formed. The dyestuffs employed in the commercial inks of to-day vary in colour from pale greenish blue to indigo and deep violet. No two give identical reactions—at all events not when mixed with the iron tannate to form the pigment in writing.

"It is owing to the difference in these provisional colouring matters that it is possible to distinguish between writing written with different kinds of ink. I was able easily to obtain samples of the inks used by the Vandams, by Mrs. Popper, by Mr. Farrington, and by the druggist. I have compared the writing of the original prescription with a colour scale of my own construction, and I have made chemical tests. The druggist's ink conforms exactly to the writing on the two pill-boxes, but not to the prescription. One of the other three inks conforms by test absolutely to the ink in that prescription signed 'Dr. C. W. H.' as a blind. In a moment my chain of evidence against the owner of that bottle of ink will be complete."

I could not help but think of the two pendulums on the shelf behind the curtain, but Craig said nothing for a moment to indicate that he referred to that apparatus. We sat dazed. Farrington seemed nervous and ill at ease. Mrs. Popper, who had not recovered from the hysterical condition of her exposure, with difficulty controlled her emotion. Vandam was crushed.

"I have not only arranged this laboratory so as to reproduce Mrs. Popper's seance-room," began Craig afresh, "but I have had the cabinet placed in relatively the same position a similar cabinet occupies in Mr. Vandam's private seance-room in the Vandam mansion.

"One night, Mr. Jameson and myself were visiting Mr. Vandam. At precisely twelve-thirty we heard most unaccountable rappings from that cabinet. I particularly noted the position of the cabinet. Back of it ran a hallway. That is duplicated here. Back of this cabinet is a hallway. I had heard of these rappings before we went, but was afraid that it would be impossible for me to catch the ghost red handed. There is a limit to what you can do the first time you enter a man's house, and, besides, that was no time to arouse suspicion in the mind of anyone. But science has a way out of every dilemma. I determined to learn something of these rappings."

Craig paused and glanced first at Farrington, then at Mrs. Popper, and then at Mr. Vandam.

"Mr. Jameson," he resumed, "will escort the doctor, the inspector, Mr. Farrington, Mrs. Popper, and Mr. Vandam into my imitation hall of the Vandam mansion. I want each of you in turn to tiptoe up that hall to a spot indicated on the wall, back of the cabinet, and strike that spot several sharp blows with your knuckles."

I did as Craig instructed tiptoeing up myself first so that they could not mistake his meaning. The rest followed separately, and after a moment we returned silently in suppressed excitement to the room.

Craig was still standing by the table, but now the pendulums with the magnets and needles and the drums worked by clockwork were before him.

"Another person outside the Vandam family had a key to the Vandam mansion," he began gravely. "That person, by the way, was the one who waited, night by night, until Mrs. Vandam took the fatal capsule, and then when she had taken it apprised the old man of the fact and strengthened an already blind faith in the shadow world."

You could have heard a pin drop. In fact you could almost have felt it drop.

"That other person who, unobserved, had free access to the house," he continued in the breathless stillness, "is in this room now."

He was looking at O'Connor as if for corroboration. O'Connor nodded. "Information derived from the butler," he muttered.

"I did not know this until yesterday," Kennedy continued, "but I suspected that something of the sort existed when I was first told by Dr. Hanson of the rappings. I determined to hear those rappings, and make a record of them. So, the night Mr. Jameson and I visited Mr. Vandam, I carried this little instrument with me."

Almost lovingly he touched the pendulums on the table. They were now at rest and kept so by means of a lever that prevented all vibration whatever.

"See, I release this lever—now, let no one in the room move. Watch the needles on the paper as the clockwork revolves the drums. I take a step—ever so lightly. The pendulums vibrate, and the needles trace a broken line on the paper on each drum. I stop; the lines are practically straight. I take another step and another, ever so lightly. See the delicate pendulums vibrate? See, the lines they trace are jagged lines."

He stripped the paper off the drums and laid it flat on the table before him, with two other similar pieces of paper.

"Just before the time of the rapping I placed this instrument in the corner of the Vandam cabinet, just as I placed it in this cabinet after Mr. Jameson conducted you from the room. In neither case were suspicions aroused. Everything in both cases was perfectly normal—I mean the 'ghost' was in ignorance of the presence, if not the very existence, of this instrument.

"This is an improved seismograph," he explained, "one after a very recent model by Prince Galitzin of the Imperial Academy of St. Petersburg. The seismograph, as you know, was devised to register earthquakes at a distance. This one not only measures the size of a distant earthquake, but the actual direction from which the earth-tremors come. That is why there are two pendulums and two drums.

"The magnetic arrangement is to cut short the vibrations set up in the pendulums, to prevent them from continuing to vibrate after the first shock. Thus they are ready in an instant to record another tremor. Other seismographs continue to vibrate for a long time as a result of one tremor only. Besides, they give little indication of the direction from which the tremors come.

"I think you must all appreciate that your tiptoeing up the hall must cause a far greater disturbance in this delicate seismograph than even a very severe earthquake thousands of miles away, which it was built to record."

He paused and examined the papers sharply.

"This is the record made by the 'ghost's' walk the other night," he said, holding up two of them in his left hand. "Here on the table, on two other longer sheets, I have records of the vibrations set up by those in this room walking to-night.

"Here is Mr. Jameson's—his is not a bit like the ghost's. Nor is Mr. Vandam's. Least of all are Dr. Hanson's and Inspector O'Connor's, for they are heavy men.

"Now here is Mr. Farrington's"—he bent down closely, "he is a light man, and the ghost was light."

Craig was playing with his victim like a cat with a mouse.

Suddenly I felt something brush by me, and with a swish of air and of garments I saw Mrs. Popper fling herself wildly at the table that bore the incriminating records. In another instant Farrington was on his feet and had made a wild leap in the same direction.

It was done so quickly that I must have acted first and thought afterward. I found myself in the midst of a melee

34

with my hand at his throat and his at mine. O'Connor with a jiu-jitsu movement bent Farrington's other arm until he released me with a cry of pain.

In front of me I saw Craig grasping Mrs. Popper's wrists as in a vise. She was glaring at him like a tigress.

"Do you suppose for a moment that that toy is going to convince the world that Henry Vandam has been deceived and that the spirit which visited him was a fraud? Is that why you have lured me here under false pretences, to play on my feelings, to insult me, to take advantage of a lone, defenceless woman, surrounded by hostile men? Shame on you," she added contemptuously. "You call yourself a gentleman, but I call you a coward."

Kennedy, always calm and collected, ignored the tirade. His voice was as cold as steel as he said: "It would do little good, Mrs. Popper, to destroy this one link in the chain I have forged. The other links are too heavy for you. Don't forget the evidence of the ink. It was your ink. Don't forget that Henry Vandam will not any longer conceal that he has altered his will in favour of you. To-night he goes from here to his lawyer's to draw up a new will altogether. Don't forget that you have caused the Vandams separately to have the prescription filled, and that you are now caught in the act of a double murder. Don't forget that you had access to the Vandam mansion, that you substituted the deadly for the harmless capsules. Don't forget that your rappings announced the death of one of your victims and urged the other, a cruelly wronged and credulous old man, to leave millions to you who had deceived and would have killed him.

"No, the record of the ghost on the seismograph was not Mr. Farrington's, as I implied at the moment when you so kindly furnished this additional proof of your guilt by trying to destroy the evidence. The ghost was you, Mrs. Popper, and you are at liberty to examine the markings as minutely as you please, but you must not destroy them. You are an astute criminal, Mrs. Popper, but to-night you are under arrest for the murder of Mary Vandam and the attempted murder of Henry Vandam."